INTO THE WOODS

by

JANE A.C. WEST AND ROGER HURN

Tribe

Book 5

To Judith – for being the best friend.

With special thanks to:

Alfie Blair
Samuel Spring
Alejandro Stone
Thomas Ward

First published in 2011 in Great Britain by
Barrington Stoke Ltd
18 Walker St, Edinburgh, EH3 7LP

www.barringtonstoke.co.uk

ISBN: 978-1-84299-603-4

Printed in China by Leo

The publisher gratefully acknowledges support from the Scottish Arts
Council towards the publication of this title.

Scottish
Arts Council

WHO ARE TRIBE?

ARE THEY HUMANS?

OR ARE THEY ANIMALS?

Tribe are humans *and* animals.

They are super-heroes with special powers.

They can *shape-shift* – change from animals to humans and back again.

THEIR PLAN: to save the world from anyone who tries to destroy it.

Tribe need to find the bad guys – before it's too late.

The Earth is in trouble – and only Tribe have the power to help.

Tribe are helped by TOK – the Tree Of Knowledge.

Tribe can travel all over the world using the roots of trees.

Tribe also have the power to talk to animals – and they can send each other mind-messages, even when they are miles apart.

CAST LIST

Finn

Bruin

Kat

Mo

Talon

Vana

and ...

Tim Burr!

Contents

Chapter 1
Forest Friends

Tribe were in their Head Quarters, a tree-house in an old oak tree. But something was wrong. The tree shivered. Its leaves quivered. The birds nesting in its branches flew away. The Tree Of Knowledge, TOK, was afraid.

Kat looked cross. "What's all the noise? I was having a cat-nap."

"This is no time for sleeping," said Vana. "Something is wrong in the forest."

"I'll go and take a bird's eye look," said Talon.

He morphed into an eagle and soared away from the tree-house.

He was back very soon.

"They're cutting down trees in the forest!" he screeched.

"There are men with huge chain-saws. What will we do if they come this way?"

"Stop them," growled Bruin.

"We'll do something *tree*-mendous!" said Finn.

"Grr," said Vana. "I'm in no mood for jokes. This is an old, old forest. No one can cut down trees here."

"Shall I tell the police?" whispered Mo.

Vana shook her head. "No! They must never know about Tribe. But we must act soon, or hundreds of trees will be killed."

"I'll stop them," snarled Bruin.

He morphed into his bear form. He was an angry mountain of thick, brown fur and long, sharp claws. He roared, showing his razor-like teeth.

"Wait! We need information first," snapped Vana. Kat – you and Mo find these people who are cutting down the trees. Find out why they have come here. Do anything you can to slow them down. Then let us know what's happened. I've got to contact someone from outside the forest ..."

"You can count on us," squeaked Mo.

"Yes, we're the *purr*-fect pair," said Kat.

Mo looked as if she wasn't so sure about that.

Chapter 2
Cat and Mouse

Kat ran swiftly through the forest. Mo scampered after her. It was odd to see a mouse chasing a cat.

Kat and Mo soon found the men with the chain-saws.

"You wait here," hissed Kat. "I'm going in to see what I can find out."

"Be careful," squeaked Mo.

"Don't worry. Cats have nine lives."

Kat trotted over to the clearing where the men were standing around a large truck.

A tall, strong man with a hard, square face stood in front of her. His eyes were cruel and cold.

"No! No! NO!" he yelled. "Don't waste time cutting down the small trees. Cut down the old trees, the big trees – they have more wood in them. I need them chopped into planks. I need a million planks of wood. My name isn't Tim Burr for nothing! Now get cutting. I love the sound of chain-saws in the morning!"

The man was looking at a map laid out
on the bonnet of the truck. Kat jumped up
on to the truck to have a look. The map
showed the forest covered with houses. The
trees had gone.

"Yuk! Get off!" yelled Tim Burr when he saw Kat. "I hate animals. And most of all I hate cats! Someone get rid of this manky moggy!"

"Yes, Boss!" shouted one of the men with a chain-saw.

He swung the chain-saw at Kat but she was too quick for him. She jumped off the truck just in time. The chain-saw sliced into the roof of the truck.

"You idiot!" yelled Tim Burr.

Kat ran over to Mo, smiling like the cat who had got the cream.

"Quick!" she hissed. "I'll send a mind message and tell the others Tim Burr wants to cut down the whole forest and put up hundreds of houses. We have to stop him now ... but we'll need help. You know where to go – and what to do."

Mo nodded once then scampered away.

Kat's green eyes glowed with anger as she glared at Tim Burr.

"You wait, Tim Burr. Tribe will cut *you* down to size!"

Chapter 3
Man Trap

Tim Burr frowned. The sky was growing very dark. What on earth was happening? He saw a huge eagle in the sky. Behind the eagle was a dark, dense cloud. But it wasn't a cloud, it was ... bees! Millions of angry bees!

"Why don't you buzz off, Tim Burr!"
called Talon as he led the bee attack on the
tree killers.

Tim Burr's men fled from the forest,
chased by the largest swarm of bees they
had ever seen. They didn't want to risk
being stung by angry bees.

"Shoo! Shoo!" squeaked Mo, jumping up
and down.

"Plan *B-ee* worked," chuckled Bruin.

Vana was howling for joy. "OK, Bruin.
Do you think you can drag those chain-saws
away and get rid of them?"

"Ready, teddy, go!" said Bruin.

He used his great strength to drag the
heavy chain-saws deep into the forest. He
dropped them into a deep hole where they
would never be found – and could never
harm another tree.

Vana chuckled. "Right, Mo. Let's get on with Plan C."

Mo scampered off, giggling to herself. She ran deep into the forest and morphed back into her human form.

Around her neck was a small, round, wooden necklace covered with odd markings. It was her secret weapon. She blew softly into the holes. A strange but sweet sound rang out through the forest. It was the Tribe secret alarm call to the animal world, asking for help.

Soon hundreds and hundreds of rabbits had arrived and formed a circle round Mo. They hated Tim Burr and all that he stood for.

"Welcome, friends," said Mo. "The forest is under attack. We have to stop Tim Burr and his men from killing the trees. We need to set a trap."

It was some hours later before Tim Burr and his men dared to return to the forest after the bee attack.

They were right to be afraid. Tribe hadn't finished with them yet.

"Come on!" yelled Tim Burr. "It's still daylight. I want to see those chain-saws cutting down more and more of those darn trees. More planks! I want MORE PLANKS!"

But suddenly ...

"Aaaagh!"

Tim Burr and his men fell into a deep hole.

It had been dug quickly and quietly by hundreds of small rabbits. They had set a man trap!

Chapter 4
Eve Earth

Tim Burr and his men were trapped in the huge pit that the rabbits had dug.

"We've got those tree-killers," said Finn. "But what do we do now?"

"Watch and learn," said Vana. "There are some people on our side – good people who want to look after the forests and the seas and the skies and the animals. I contacted the reporter Eve Earth. She's on her way now. She'll tell the world what Tim Burr tried to do here."

Far away they heard the sound of police cars. Leading the police into the forest was a woman with wild, curly hair. She was carrying a camera, a notepad and a microphone.

"This way, officers," she said. "Tim Burr is cutting down these huge old trees. It's against the law. There he is! Arrest that man! Lock him up!"

"This way, sir," said a burly police officer.

He pulled Tim Burr out of the pit and put a pair of handcuffs on him. "You won't be seeing any trees for a long time – just a lot of bars."

"Do you have anything to say?" said Eve Earth, pushing a microphone into Tim Burr's face.

"Get off me!" snapped Tim Burr. "This is all a mistake. I've done nothing!"

"Then who cut down all these trees?" smiled Eve Earth.

"Er ... beavers!" said Tim Burr.

Vana had to smile. Tim Burr was as bright as a broken light-bulb.

"Beavers. I'll make a note of that," said Eve Earth. "One last question, Mr Burr – where did the beavers get the chain-saws?"

Tim Burr was silent. He was led off and pushed into the back of a police car and driven away out of the forest.

Tribe vanished back into the forest as silently as they had come. As for Tim Burr, you might say he couldn't see the wood for the trees!

BARK WORSE THAN BITE

Cutting trees down without a permit is a big problem all over the world. It's called illegal logging.

Hard-wood trees, like teak, come from tropical rain forests. This includes countries like Ghana in Africa, Brazil in South America, and Indonesia in Asia.

Teak is a hard and oily wood. If you put it outside it will not rot away. Decking and garden furniture are made from teak and last a long time. It is very popular. But teak trees grow very slowly so the wood costs a lot to buy. Some people break the law and cut down trees to make more money.

Millions of acres of rain forest are destroyed every year in this way.

If you want to find out more, go to www.fsc.org.

TALON - EAGLE BOY

VANA'S TWiN BROTHER.

STRONG-WiLLED AND LOYAL.

SPECiAL SKiLL: amazing eye-sight.

LOVES: flying, mountains.

HATES: being grounded.

MOST LiKELY TO SAY: "Vana's right!"

BiGGEST SECRET: wishes he was

Tribe's leader.

TRIBE TALK!

To:	Talon
From:	Henry
Subject:	Teak

Dear Talon,

My mum and dad want to buy some garden furniture made out of teak. What can I do?

Henry

To:	Henry
From:	Talon
Subject:	Re: Teak

Hi, Henry,

Tell them that lots of teak furniture is made from illegal logging. They can check that their furniture is made from legal wood by making sure the Forest Stewardship Council says it's OK.

Gotta fly,

Talon

FYI: EAGLES

 • Eagles have very good eye-sight. This is what we mean when we say someone is "eagle eyed".

 • Eagles eat small animals like mice and rabbits.

• Golden Eagles are large birds. They have a wing-span of over two metres.

• Golden Eagles nest in high places like cliffs. They don't like living near humans.

• An adult Golden Eagle is not attacked or eaten by any other animal. They are only at risk from humans.

• Don't tell Talon, but female Golden Eagles are larger than the males.

JOKE OF THE DAY

TALON: What's the difference between an eagle and a post-box?

MO: I don't know ...

TALON: In that case, I won't let you post my letters!

CHECK OUT THE REST OF THE TRIBE BOOKS!

For more info check out our website:
www.barringtonstoke.co.uk